101 Jungle Stories

MOONSTONE

Published in Moonstone
by Rupa Publications India Pvt. Ltd 2025
161-B/4, Gulmohar House,
Yusuf Sarai Community Centre,
New Delhi 110049

Sales centres:
Bengaluru Chennai
Hyderabad Kolkata Mumbai

P-ISBN: 978-93-7003-770-0
E-ISBN: 978-93-7003-534-8

First impression 2025

10 9 8 7 6 5 4 3 2 1

Printed in India

Contents

Contents

1. The Leopard's Lovely Cakes

Luma the leopard lived in a cosy cottage at the edge of the jungle. She wore a pink apron, had sparkly eyes, and baked the most beautiful cakes anyone had ever seen. Her cakes were soft, sweet, and shaped like flowers and hearts. Every weekend, Luma set up a little stall near the river. Animals lined up, smiling, to buy her treats. But Luma never kept the money. She gave it all to help old turtles, lost cubs, and hungry birds. One day, the jungle animals surprised her with a big thank-you party and a golden whisk! Luma beamed. She knew kindness was the best recipe of all. From then on, Luma baked with even more love.

2. Lost and Found Friends

Ellie, the little elephant, loved to explore the jungle. One day, she wandered too far while chasing butterflies. Suddenly, she looked around and could not see her home! Ellie's big floppy ears drooped, and tears rolled down her cheeks. She sat on a rock and cried, feeling very small and scared. Just then, a group of tiny, colourful birds flew over. They chirped happily and circled around Ellie. 'Don't worry!' they sang. The birds led Ellie through the soft green trees, flying ahead like little bright lights. Soon, Ellie saw her family waiting and waving their trunks! Ellie ran to them with joy. She learned that friends can be found in the most surprising ways.

3. The Secret Treehouse

Leo the lion cub loved to explore the jungle. One sunny afternoon, while chasing a butterfly, he bumped into a huge old tree. Curious, Leo pushed aside some vines and found a hidden ladder inside the tree! With his little backpack bouncing, he carefully climbed up. At the top, Leo discovered a secret treehouse with soft pillows, wooden shelves, and shining windows! He looked out and saw the whole jungle like a big green sea. Leo cheered and made the treehouse his new secret place to read, dream, and nap. He learnt that magical surprises can be hidden all around if you just keep looking. And every climb brought a new adventure!

4. The Waterfall Map

Penny the parrot loved flying high above the jungle. One day, a strong wind blew her map right out of her claws! It floated down and landed near Daisy, a young, curious deer, who was drinking water at a small waterfall. Daisy picked up the colourful, torn map with her nose. She saw shining lines leading to something exciting! Penny swooped down, looking worried. 'Is this yours?' Daisy asked kindly. Penny nodded happily. Together, they followed the map across sparkling streams and sunny hills. At the end, they found a hidden pond full of sweet fruits and flowers! From that day, Daisy and Penny became the best of friends, sharing adventures and laughter every day.

5.   Fireflies at Night

Tommy the tiny turtle loved quiet walks under the stars. One evening, he noticed blinking golden lights dancing across the field. Curious, Tommy slowly followed them, his little feet padding softly on the grass. The lights floated ahead, twinkling and spinning like tiny stars. Suddenly, Tommy reached a clearing and gasped — all his friends were there! The fireflies had led him to a surprise party just for him! There were colourful flowers, juicy fruits, and happy laughter everywhere. Tommy's shell shone under the soft glow of the fireflies. He smiled the biggest smile and knew he was loved. That night, Tommy learnt that sometimes the tiniest lights lead to the brightest happiness.

6. Bridge Over Crocodiles

Freddy the frog loved adventures more than anything. One bright morning, he found a wobbly old bridge hanging over a wide river. Below, the water swirled in big blue circles, and cheeky crocodiles floated with wide grins. Freddy's heart beat fast, but he took a deep breath. 'I can do this!' he said to himself. Carefully, he hopped onto the first plank, which creaked loudly. He jumped again and again, each plank shaking under his little green feet. The crocodiles chuckled and clapped their tails, cheering him on. With one final big leap, Freddy made it safely across! He turned around and laughed with the crocodiles. Freddy learnt that being brave can lead to the happiest surprises

7. The Jungle King's Crown

Lulu, the little leopard, loved to run and play in the jungle. One bright afternoon, while chasing butterflies, she tumbled into a pile of soft leaves. As she shook the dust from her fur, something shiny caught her eye. There, half-buried among the leaves, was a golden glittery crown! Her eyes grew huge with wonder. The crown sparkled brightly under the warm sunlight. Lulu smiled and placed it gently on her head, giggling. She had found the Jungle King's lost treasure! From that day, Lulu became the jungle's little queen.

8. The Jungle Teamwork

In the heart of a bright green jungle, four friends had a plan. Milo the monkey spotted a huge mango hanging high in a tree. 'Let's get it down!' he called. Polly the parrot flew up, flapping excitedly. Below, Ella the elephant and Tilly the tiny bear held a big leaf, ready to catch the fruit. Milo swung from the branch and gave the mango a little tug. It wobbled... then dropped! 'Got it!' shouted Ella, as the mango landed safely on the leaf. Everyone cheered and laughed. They all sat under the tree, sharing the juicy mango. It tasted extra sweet because they worked together. From that day on, they knew, with teamwork, anything was possible in the jungle!

9. Fifi Saves the Jamun Tree

Fifi, the flamingo, loved reading books while perched in her favourite jamun tree. The thick branches of the jamun tree provided shade, and the gentle breeze was ideal for reading. Every day, she'd perch up high with a story in her wings. One morning, loud chopping sounds echoed through the jungle. Tree-cutters had come with big saws to cut down the jamun trees! Fifi's heart sank. 'Not my tree!' she cried. She quickly flew to her friends – Coco the clever crow, and Tara the strong tiger. Together, they gathered more animals and formed a big circle around the trees. They hugged the trunks tightly and shouted, 'Save our trees!' The tree-cutters stopped. They listened. And they left. Fifi had saved her reading tree — with friendship and courage.

10. The Glowing Flower Quest

Nina the nightingale loved stories about magic. One evening, she heard an old tale about a glowing flower hidden deep in the jungle. With a brave heart, Nina spread her shiny wings and flew out into the night. The stars twinkled above, and the trees whispered secrets as she searched. Hour after hour, she fluttered through misty woods and over sparkling streams. Just as the first light of dawn touched the sky, Nina saw a soft golden glow beneath a great old tree. There, blooming gently, was the glowing flower! Nina sang a sweet song of joy as the jungle woke up around her. She learnt that hope and patience always lead to the most beautiful rewards.

11. The Turtle Rescue

Tom the tiger was strong and brave, but also very gentle. One evening, as he walked along the riverbank, he heard soft cries. Looking down, he saw a group of tiny turtles stuck in the hot, shifting sand. The river was just ahead, but the little turtles were too small to make it on their own. Without wasting a moment, Tom knelt down and carefully lifted them onto his broad back. Step by step, he padded across the soft sand until they reached the cool, flowing river. The turtles slid happily into the water, waving their tiny flippers. Tom roared softly with pride. That evening, he learnt that true strength is shown by helping those who are smaller and weaker.

12. The Parrot's Clever Clues

Polly the parrot loved to chatter and sing. One morning, she spotted her friend Sam the snake looking very lost in the thick jungle. 'Turn left, Sam! Slither straight! Now right!' Polly shouted from the top of a tall tree. Sam listened carefully, his tongue flicking happily as he followed Polly's funny directions. Around twisty roots and under leafy branches, he wriggled, always trusting Polly's clever clues. At last, Sam reached the sunny clearing where all his friends were waiting for a picnic! Everyone cheered, and Sam gave Polly a happy wiggle of thanks. Polly flapped her wings proudly. That day, they all learnt that a little kindness and clear words can guide friends safely home.

13. The Shy Sloth's Smile

Sally the sloth was very shy. She spent most of her days hanging upside-down on a quiet tree, watching the jungle with big, slow blinks. She hardly ever smiled. One soft, sunny afternoon, as Sally dozed, a tiny bright butterfly fluttered close. Gently, it landed right on the tip of her nose! Sally opened one eye, wriggled her nose, and let out a tiny giggle. Then another! Soon, she was laughing so sweetly that even the trees seemed to sway with joy. Other animals peeked out, smiling too. That day, Sally learnt that even the smallest, softest things could bring big happiness. And from then on, a little smile always played on her gentle face.

14. Monkey Mischief

Max the monkey loved playing tricks. One bright afternoon, while Sam the sloth was napping under a big banana tree, Max tiptoed close and snatched Sam's colourful hat! With a cheeky grin, Max raced away, swinging through the trees. Sam woke up, rubbed his eyes, and saw Max's tail disappearing into the leaves. 'Hey, come back!' Sam shouted, but he was already laughing. Slowly but surely, Sam gave chase, while Max giggled from the branches above. After lots of running, swinging, and tumbling, Max finally dropped the hat gently onto Sam's head. Both friends fell into a fit of giggles under the tree. That day, they learnt that a little bit of harmless fun can make the best memories.

15. The Gentle Tiger

Timmy the tiger was the biggest animal in the jungle, but he had the softest heart. One bright morning, while strolling through the bushes, he heard a tiny bleat. Following the sound, Timmy found a little lamb lost and scared among the tall green leaves. The lamb shivered, looking very small and alone. Timmy bent down gently and gave a loud but friendly roar, 'Come home!' The lamb's ears perked up, and it smiled. Walking carefully, Timmy guided the little lamb through the jungle paths. Soon, they reached the lamb's meadow where its family waited. Everyone cheered for Timmy! That day, Timmy learnt that real strength lies not in fear but in kindness and a caring heart.

16. Swinging High!

Ella the elephant was always curious about jungle games. One breezy afternoon, she watched a group of lively lemurs leaping and swinging from thick jungle vines. Their laughter filled the air, and Ella's heart tickled with excitement. Nervously, she wrapped her trunk around a strong vine. The lemurs cheered, 'Come on, Ella!' With a big breath, she lifted her feet and swung! At first, she wobbled, but then she swung higher and higher, feeling the wind rush past her ears. The lemurs bounced and laughed all around her, glowing bright against the soft grey jungle. That day, Ella learnt that trying new things could lead to wonderful fun and that friends make every swing even sweeter.

17. The Trapped Baby Elephant

In the middle of the jungle, Baby Bobo the elephant was having a grand time splashing in puddles. But suddenly, one deep, muddy puddle trapped him! He tried to wriggle and push, but he was stuck fast. Seeing Bobo in trouble, the jungle animals quickly gathered around. Tiny birds chirped encouragement, frogs hopped excitedly, and even big lions lent their strong shoulders. 'Push, everyone!' chirped the parrot. Working together, they pushed and pulled with all their might. At last, with a happy squelch, Bobo popped free, landing with a splash that soaked everyone! They all cheered and laughed. That day, Bobo learnt that no matter how sticky a problem, friends who work together can set you free.

18. Race with a Cheetah Cub

Charlie the cheetah cub loved to race anything that moved. One sunny afternoon, he saw Penny the parrot fluttering from tree to tree. With a playful grin, Charlie called out, 'Race you to the river!' Penny laughed and flapped her wings as fast as she could. Charlie dashed across the grassy ground, his paws flying, while Penny zoomed above him, her feathers flashing. Trees and bushes blurred past them in a whirl of green. Just before the river's edge, Penny swooped low and touched the finish line first! Both friends tumbled into giggles. That day, Charlie learnt that sometimes speed isn't everything — and laughing with your friends makes every race a win.

19. The Jungle Talent Show

One bright morning, the jungle buzzed with excitement — it was the day of the Jungle Talent Show! Pippa the panther was the first to step onto the grassy stage. She grinned and began juggling three big coconuts high into the air, her tail twitching proudly. Next came Benny the bear, a round and jolly fellow, who banged out a happy tune on bamboo drums. His paws moved so fast, the jungle shook with laughter! Monkeys clapped, birds sang along, and even turtles tapped their feet. Colourful musical notes floated all around like butterflies. That day, Pippa, Benny, and all their friends learnt that sharing your special talents brings everyone joy — and makes wonderful memories too.

20. Night-Time Jungle Tales

Every evening, as the jungle grew quiet and the stars twinkled above, Oliver the wise old owl flew to his favourite branch. Below him, monkeys, tigers, rabbits, and even tiny frogs gathered in a cosy circle. They all looked up with bright, excited eyes. Oliver fluffed his feathers, cleared his throat, and began to hoot wonderful stories of magic rivers, golden trees, and brave little ants. The jungle glowed softly under the purple sky, and a gentle breeze carried his words far and wide. Smiles grew bigger with every tale. That night, and every night after, the animals learnt that the best adventures sometimes live in the stories shared together under the stars.

21. The Flower Fairy

One warm morning, Tina the tiger cub wandered deeper into the jungle than ever before. Sunlight danced on the leaves, and soft breezes carried the sweet smell of flowers. Suddenly, a flash of gold caught her eye. Curious, Tina tiptoed closer and found a bright golden flower blooming in a quiet clearing. Peeking inside, she gasped in wonder — curled up in the heart of the flower was a tiny, glowing fairy, fast asleep! Her wings shimmered like sunshine. Tina smiled widely but stayed very still, not wanting to wake her. That day, Tina learnt that magic hides in the quietest corners, and sometimes, the gentlest moments bring the greatest joy.

22. The Wishing Vine

One sunny morning, Poppy the parrot found a strange vine twisting up a tall jungle tree. It shimmered in the sunlight and swayed even when the breeze was still. Feeling curious, Poppy tugged the vine gently with her beak. Suddenly, there was a loud rustle — and to Poppy's amazement, sweet golden bananas began to rain down from the trees! They fell like little golden drops of sunshine. Poppy flapped her wings joyfully, giggling as the bananas bounced all around her. Soon, all her jungle friends gathered to share the treat. That day, Poppy learnt that sometimes, a little bit of courage to tug at the unknown can bring the sweetest surprises.

23. The Invisible Panther

Shadow the panther was the cheekiest animal in the whole jungle. He had a special trick — he could hide so well that no one could ever spot him! One sunny afternoon, as the other animals played near the banana trees, Shadow suddenly vanished into thin air. 'Where did he go?' cried the parrots. 'Did he disappear?' gasped the monkeys. Everyone looked around in confusion. Suddenly, 'Peekaboo!' Shadow leapt out from behind the banana leaves, his eyes twinkling, and he had a huge grin on his face. All the animals burst into laughter! That day, they learnt that a little bit of mystery and a lot of laughter could make even the hottest afternoons full of magic and fun.

24. Whispering Trees

Ben the bear was small but full of dreams. Some days, he felt brave enough to chase butterflies, and some days, he just wanted a quiet cuddle. One cool, dark evening, he found a tall glowing tree standing in the middle of the jungle. It looked so kind and strong. Ben wrapped his little arms around the glowing trunk. To his surprise, he heard a soft whisper, 'Be brave, little one.' Ben's heart filled with warmth and courage. Tiny glowing words floated into the starry sky like little fireflies. That night, Ben learnt that sometimes, a simple hug can whisper the strongest magic — and bravery often grows from the gentlest places.

25. The Talking Lizard

Lucy the lizard was the most colourful creature in the jungle. One bright morning, as a group of little animal explorers wandered through the woods, Lucy clicked her tongue loudly. 'Follow me!' she laughed, her tail flicking with excitement. With a cheeky grin, she zipped ahead, leading the way along a twisting, turning jungle path splattered with puddles of bright flowers and buzzing butterflies. Her shiny, spotty skin sparkled in the sunlight like a rainbow. The little explorers raced after her, giggling and slipping through the colourful splashes. That day, they learnt that adventures are even more magical when you follow someone full of laughter, colour, and a little bit of mischief!

26. The Secret Mushroom Door

Sam the squirrel loved finding secret places. One bright morning, while scampering through the jungle, he spotted a patch of big, red-spotted mushrooms. They looked like little umbrellas! Curious, Sam poked one gently with his paw. To his amazement, the mushroom wobbled, creaked, and swung open like a tiny door! Behind it was a glowing world full of candy canes, jellybean bushes, and gumdrop hills. Sam's eyes grew wide with wonder. He dashed inside, nibbling a lollipop tree and sliding down a sugar slide. That day, Sam learnt that adventure often hides behind the most unexpected doors — and sometimes, the sweetest worlds are waiting just one brave push away!

27. The Jungle Crown

Dina, the deer, was gentle and kind and loved by all in the jungle. One bright afternoon, the animals gathered in a clearing with a special surprise. They had crafted a crown from green leaves, red berries, and soft feathers. Dina's eyes sparkled as they placed it gently on her head. The monkeys clapped, the parrots sang, and even the lions gave joyful roars. Dina blushed but stood proud, her heart glowing with joy. From that day on, she became the jungle's kind queen, guiding all with care and warmth. She learnt that true queens wear not just crowns of leaves and feathers — but of kindness, love, and a heart big enough for everyone.

28. Flying Carpet Ride

Milo the monkey loved finding new things hidden in the jungle. One afternoon, near the roots of an old banyan tree, he discovered a colourful carpet rolled up neatly. Curious, he gave it a shake — and WHOOSH! The carpet rose into the air, lifting Milo high above the trees! He whooped and waved his arms, sailing over bright green leaves, colourful flowers, and sparkling rivers. Birds chirped and monkeys cheered from below. The jungle looked like a big, beautiful painting from up high. Milo learnt that sometimes, the wildest dreams could come true when you find a little bit of magic hidden in unexpected places — and when you are brave enough to hold on tight!

29. The Rainbow Rain

One quiet afternoon, the jungle sky turned a funny shade of purple. The animals looked up with wide, wondering eyes. Drip, drop — the first raindrops fell, but they were not plain water! Instead, splashes of bright red, blue, green, and yellow rained down like magic paint! Trees caught the colours and turned into beautiful, glowing rainbows. Monkeys spun and danced, lions pranced, and birds twirled in the bright drops. Soon, the whole jungle looked like a giant, happy painting. That day, the animals learnt that surprises can fill the world with joy, and even a rainy day can become a celebration when you laugh, dance, and welcome all the colours of life!

30. The Unicorn Zebra

Zara the zebra always felt a little different. Her stripes shone a little brighter, and her eyes twinkled a little more. One misty morning, as she splashed in a dewy meadow, Zara felt a tickle on her forehead. She looked into the river's mirror and gasped — a tiny, sparkling rainbow horn peeked out between her ears! All the animals gathered around, cheering and dancing with joy. Zara smiled proudly, her heart glowing brighter than ever. She realised that being different was her magic. That day, Zara learnt that true beauty shines when you embrace your special self, and sometimes, the most magical things grow right from the places you least expect.

31. The Missing Fruit Mystery

Pepe the parrot loved bananas more than anything. Every morning, he counted his golden fruits with great care. But one sunny morning, he gasped — the bananas had vanished! Pepe scratched his head, looking around with wide, puzzled eyes. From behind thick, leafy bushes, tiny giggles floated through the air. Pepe flew closer and spotted a group of cheeky monkeys tossing his bananas back and forth, laughing and swinging wildly!

Pepe couldn't help but laugh too. He joined the silly game, flapping and chasing after his bouncing bananas. That day, Pepe learnt that sometimes mysteries are just games waiting to be played — and sharing laughter is much sweeter than keeping all the bananas to yourself.

32. The Lost Jungle Drums

Bella the bear loved jungle music more than honey! One day, the drumming stopped. The jungle felt too quiet. Bella looked around and realised the jungle drums were gone! She searched behind trees, under rocks, and through tall bushes. Just as she was about to give up, she spotted a patch of bright green ferns dancing in the wind. She tiptoed closer and gently brushed the leaves aside. There they were — the shining, colourful jungle drums, safe and sound! Bella gave a big, happy roar and beat the drums with joy. The jungle buzzed with music again. That day, Bella learnt that with a little patience and curiosity, lost things often lead to the happiest discoveries.

33. The Riddle Waterfall

Ruby the rabbit loved solving tricky puzzles. One day, she came upon a big waterfall splashing loudly in the heart of the jungle. On a shiny stone nearby, a riddle was carved: 'I open when you say the truth.' Ruby thought carefully, then smiled and whispered, 'I believe in magic.' At once, the waterfall shimmered and split in two! Behind the curtain of water, a glowing cave appeared, filled with gold, jewels, and rainbow sparkles. Ruby's eyes widened in wonder. But instead of keeping it all, she called her jungle friends and shared the treasure. Soon, everyone had what they needed — warm homes, full bellies, and joyful hearts. That day, Ruby learnt that true magic grows when shared.

34. The Jungle Maze

Max the monkey loved exploring new places, especially when they looked tricky! One day, he found a leafy maze hidden deep in the jungle. The walls were high with twisty vines curling in all directions. Max stepped in happily, but after many turns, he felt lost. 'Oh no!' he said. Just then, the vines began to wiggle gently. One vine curved like an arrow, pointing to the left. Another dropped low like a rope. Max's eyes lit up — the vines were helping him! Swinging and skipping, Max followed the green hints until he burst out into the sunshine. That day, he learnt that sometimes nature itself becomes your guide when you listen with joy and a brave heart.

35. The Glowing Flower Hunt

Tiny the tiger loved finding secret treasures hidden deep in the jungle. One evening, when the sky turned soft and dusky, he tiptoed through thick, leafy vines. The jungle felt cool and whispery. Suddenly, in a quiet corner, Tiny spotted a soft, golden glow. His heart thumped with excitement! Creeping closer, he found a beautiful golden flower, shining warmly like a little sun. Tiny gasped with wonder and sat down gently beside it, feeling calm and happy. That night, Tiny learnt that patience and quiet steps often lead to the brightest discoveries, and that sometimes, magic blooms where no one else dares to look.

36. The Acorn Surprise

One sunny morning, Benny the bunny and Suri the squirrel were playing near their jungle treehouse when Benny spotted something peeking out of an old log. 'Look!' Benny gasped, pointing with his paw. 'It's a giant acorn!' Suri scampered over, her eyes wide. 'That's not just any acorn,' she whispered. 'It's the jungle king's golden acorn!' They gently rolled the log open. Inside, nestled in moss, sat a golden-striped acorn glowing softly. 'We must return it,' Benny said bravely. They carried it through winding trails and leafy tunnels until they reached the ancient oak. As they placed it beneath its roots, a breeze whooshed past. 'Thank you, little ones,' the wind seemed to whisper. And just like that, the jungle sparkled with magic again.

37. The Lost Locket

Leo the lion cub loved to pretend he was an explorer. One quiet afternoon, while playing near the jungle rocks, he spotted something shiny peeking out from under thick green moss. Curious, he brushed it away with his paw and gasped — it was an old golden locket! Gently, he opened it and found a tiny picture inside of another lion, wearing a brave smile. Leo felt a warm feeling in his chest. 'An explorer, just like me,' he whispered. That day, Leo learnt that treasures aren't always gold and gems — sometimes, they're stories from the past, waiting quietly for someone to remember them with wonder.

38. The Vanishing Footprints

Tina, the tiger cub, loved following tracks through the jungle. One morning, she spotted a line of tiny muddy footprints and giggled with excitement. 'Someone's off on an adventure!' she whispered, and quickly began to follow. The trail zigzagged between trees, around bushes, and through tall grass. But just as she reached the river, the prints stopped. Splash! A swirl of water glimmered, but the footprints were gone. Tina sat at the river's edge, blinking in surprise. Then she smiled — some stories, she thought, love to stay a mystery. That day, Tina learnt that not all trails need an ending, and sometimes, the fun is in the chase.

39. The Secret Animal Meeting

When the jungle fell silent and stars twinkled gently above, a soft breeze whispered through the banyan trees. Beneath the biggest one, four animals gathered quietly — Felix the fox, Olive the owl, Bruno the bear, and Momo the monkey. They didn't speak loudly or shout; instead, they shared stories, dreams, and jungle secrets in soft voices. The moonlight poured gently through the thick branches, casting glowing shadows all around. Every rustle, every hoot felt like part of a magical hush. That night, they learnt that the quietest moments often hold the deepest friendships, and that secrets shared under moonlight feel like stardust in your heart.

40. The Crystal Cave

Maya the monkey was chasing butterflies when she slipped behind a thick curtain of vines. 'Oof!' she giggled, tumbling into a hidden cave. Her eyes widened — the walls sparkled like stars! Crystals of every colour glowed gently, casting rainbow patterns that danced across the stone. Maya gasped in delight and twirled beneath the shimmering lights. Every step echoed with twinkles. It felt like walking inside a rainbow. She picked a small crystal to keep, its glow soft and warm in her paw. That day, Maya learnt that the most beautiful surprises often wait quietly, hidden behind the smallest twists and turns.

41. Birthday in the Jungle

Tina the tiger woke up and stretched. Something was different. The jungle was very quiet. She walked outside her leafy den—and surprise! Her friends were waiting! The elephant, the monkey, the parrot, and the turtle all shouted, 'Happy Birthday, Tina!' There were balloons in the trees and party hats on everyone's heads. A big cake made from yummy fruit sat on a log. The candles were glowing. Tina smiled widely. She didn't know her friends remembered her birthday! They sang songs, clapped, and danced in the jungle. Tina felt happy and loved. That day, she learnt that birthdays are special when your friends are with you. The jungle felt just like a big, warm hug.

42. The Great Jungle Dance

The jungle was buzzing with excitement. It was time for the Great Jungle Dance! Monkeys juggled coconuts while swinging from vines. Parrots twirled in the air, their feathers spinning like fans. Elephants stomped rhythmically, making the ground bounce with joy. Frogs leapt, tigers swayed, and even shy sloths tapped their toes. Leaves twirled in the air like confetti, and laughter filled the trees. Birds beat their wings like drums. The whole jungle clapped, cheered, and joined in. That day, everyone learnt that dancing isn't about being perfect — it's about moving with joy, together. The jungle sang with celebration, and every animal—big or small—felt the rhythm of happiness deep in their heart.

The jungle was buzzing with busy paws, claws, and wings. A big celebration was coming! Ellie the elephant dipped her paintbrush into bright colours and painted thick green vines in swirly patterns. Parrots flew by, tying bunches of flowers to branches, giggling as petals floated down. Tigers helped hang leafy garlands while monkeys tossed fruits into colourful piles. Butterflies zipped past, adding sparkle to every corner. Soon, the whole jungle glowed with colour—reds, yellows, blues, and greens! Ellie looked around and smiled. That day, she learnt that when everyone works together, even the wildest jungle can become the most beautiful place. The forest didn't just look bright—it felt full of joy.

44. The Musical Parade

Bongo the bear marched proudly, beating his big jungle drum. Boom, boom, boom! Just above, Polly the parrot soared, singing cheerful tunes that twirled through the treetops. Close behind came Ellie the elephant, her trunk swaying to the beat, and Momo the monkey, happily shaking his maraca with a giggle. Alongside them, two green frogs thumped tiny pots, adding their own thumpy-thump rhythm to the melody. The jungle trail sparkled with sounds and colours. Flowers bobbed, trees leaned in, and every leaf seemed to hum along. Even the shiest creatures peeked out to listen. With each joyful step, the music grew louder, brighter, happier. That day, Bongo realised something big—when animals play together, the whole jungle sings.

45. The Colour Festival

It was time for the Jungle Colour Festival! Baskets of juicy berries were ready — blueberries, strawberries, mangoes, and more. The animals dipped their paws, wings, and tails into the bright paints and splashed them everywhere! The tiger turned blue, the snake turned pink, and the owl was suddenly bright yellow! Everyone ran through the trees, laughing and dripping in colour. Little pawprints covered the ground like a rainbow path. No one was clean, and no one cared. That day, they learnt that being messy could be beautiful, and the best fun was shared with friends. The jungle didn't just look brighter — it felt full of laughter and joy.

Milo the Red Panda waited all year for the jungle's most magical night. As the sun dipped low, animals gathered in the clearing, each holding a small lantern made of leaves, vines, and glowing fruits. When the moon rose high, Milo took a deep breath and let his lantern go. It floated up, soft and golden, joining hundreds of twinkling lights in the sky. Stars shimmered above, and the jungle below sparkled with gentle glows. Everyone watched in wonder. That night, Milo learnt that light doesn't just come from the stars—it also shines from hearts that share dreams. And as lanterns rose higher, the jungle glowed like a golden dream.

47. The Moonlight Party

Fifi the frog loved dancing, especially when no one was watching. One quiet night, with the moon shining high, she leapt from lily pad to lily pad, twirling with joy. Suddenly, tiny lights blinked all around her — fireflies! They lit up the jungle floor like twinkling stars. The puddles shimmered silver, and Fifi spun in the soft glow, giggling. More animals peeked out and joined in — hopping, swaying, laughing under the moon. That night, Fifi learnt that joy shines brightest when shared, and even the quietest jungle corners can come alive when laughter meets light.

48. Jungle Olympics

The Jungle Olympics had begun! Leo the lion crouched low, tail twitching, and dashed across the field like lightning. Tina, the tiger, leapt onto the nearest tree and climbed so fast that her stripes became blurry. Max the monkey whooshed from vine to vine, flipping and laughing through the air. All around, animals clapped, cheered, and waved leafy flags. The jungle floor buzzed with excitement as each event brought more fun and more giggles. In the end, no one counted medals. Everyone was a winner for trying their best. That day, they learnt that it isn't about who's fastest — it's about cheering, trying, and enjoying the race together.

32

49. The Jungle Feast

It was the day of the Great Jungle Feast! Ellie the elephant picked the ripest fruits from tall trees, using her trunk like a basket. The parrots flapped and fluttered, stirring big pots of bubbling soup with wooden spoons. Monkeys peeled bananas, turtles arranged berries, and bears brought juicy melons. Soon, a long table made of jungle logs stood covered with delicious dishes—fruit pies, warm soups, sweet honey drops, and more. The animals sat side by side, sharing, laughing, and tasting every bite. That day, they learnt that food tastes better when made together. And in the heart of the forest, their big, happy feast filled the jungle with warmth, cheer, and full tummies.

50. The Raft Party

Benny the wolf had a bright idea — 'Let's have a raft party!' he howled with glee. With logs, vines, and lots of laughter, he and his best friends — Fifi the fox, Bubbles the bear, Ruby the rabbit, and Poppy the parrot — built a sturdy raft together. When it was ready, they set sail down the sparkling river beneath the green jungle canopy.

Bubbles held a pink flower he'd picked for the ride, and Ruby brought snacks in her little pouch. Fifi told funny stories, and Poppy chirped cheerful tunes. The raft bobbed gently, surrounded by dragonflies and blooming flowers.

They didn't need roads, plans, or even a map — just friendship, sunlight, and a river that carried their giggles along.

51. The Flying Foal

In a quiet jungle glade, a baby horse named Kibi sighed as he watched birds soar above the trees. 'I wish I could fly too,' he whispered. Just then, a soft sparkle floated down—a jungle fairy! With a gentle laugh, she tapped Kibi's back. Poof! Two shiny wings sprouted. 'You've been kind and curious, Kibi,' she said. 'Now you may fly!' Kibi neighed with delight and flapped his feathery wings. Whoosh! Up he soared, past parrots, butterflies, and rainbow clouds. Monkeys waved, and frogs gasped in awe. He swooped and twirled, his hooves dancing in the sky. From that day on, Kibi wasn't just a foal—he was the jungle's first flying wonder!

52. Building a Jungle Shelter

Dark clouds gathered, and rain began to fall fast. Penny the parrot flapped her wings and called out, 'Quick! Let's build a shelter!' She found big jungle leaves and helped press them together between tree trunks. Max the monkey held branches, Tina the tiger fetched vines, and the turtles stacked stones. Together, they made a cosy leafy hut just in time. As the rain poured outside, all the animals snuggled close, dry and warm inside their jungle shelter. Laughter echoed under the green roof. That day, they learnt that working together turns storms into stories. The rain didn't feel scary anymore — it felt like music on their leafy home.

53. Meerkat and Warthog Chase

Milo the meerkat peeked over a rock, spotting his friend Wally the warthog munching on jungle roots. With a cheeky grin, Milo scurried up, poked Wally's back, and squeaked, 'Catch me if you can!' Wally snorted with surprise and bounded after him, giggling. Milo darted between bushes, zipped over logs, and wiggled into tiny tunnels. Wally puffed along behind, hooves thudding and tail wagging. Leaves flew! Dust swirled! The chase was wild and silly. Finally, both tumbled into a heap, rolling with laughter. That day, they learnt that the best games need no toys—just sunshine, friends, and a little bit of mischief.

54. The Quicksand Rescue

Ellie the elephant was walking through a quiet jungle path when squelch!—her foot sank into soft, sticky ground. 'Oh no!' she cried. It was quicksand! The more she wriggled, the deeper she sank. But before panic could set in, her jungle friends came rushing. Max the monkey grabbed a vine, Polly the peacock shouted directions, and Leo the lion tugged with all his might. Together, they pulled and heaved until Ellie popped out with a loud slurp! Everyone tumbled backwards, giggling with relief. That day, Ellie learnt that even sticky trouble can be solved with teamwork, clever thinking, and friends who never let go.

55. The Panther Cub's Fear

A tiny panther cub tiptoed through the shadowy jungle, his eyes wide and tail tucked low. Strange night sounds echoed—rustling leaves, distant hoots, and a sudden splash! He whimpered softly and crouched beside a tree, shivering. Just then, a gentle owl fluttered down, her feathers glowing softly in the moonlight. She wrapped her wings around him and whispered, 'You're safe, little one.' The panther snuggled close, his whiskers twitching, and let out a quiet purr. That night, he learnt that even the darkest forest feels warmer when someone kind sits beside you. Fear faded, and in its place came calm, and cuddles under a starry sky.

56. The Cave of Bats

Bella the bear was exploring when she saw a cave. Curious, she tiptoed inside. It was cold and quiet... until—squeak, squeak! A burst of wings fluttered above her head! Bats! Bella gasped, stumbled back, and squealed. But then... she noticed the bats weren't scary at all. They looped and twirled like dancers, their wings glittering in the dim light. Bella giggled. 'You're just tiny jungle dancers!' she said, smiling wide. That day, she learnt that fear can turn into laughter when we look a little closer. As she waved goodbye to her new bat friends, Bella felt proud — and brave. Monkeys found mangoes. Shared with parrot, turtle, and tiger!

57. Saving the Jungle

One hot afternoon, tiny flames began to spread through the jungle grass. 'Fire!' shouted Ruby the rabbit. She grabbed a bucket and dashed to the stream. Her best friend, Squeaky the squirrel, joined in. Together, they filled their buckets and splashed water over the flames. Splash! Splash! More animals arrived, passing buckets from paw to paw. The fire crackled, but the animals didn't stop. Ruby and Squeaky worked side by side, smiling as they soaked the flames. Slowly, the fire sizzled out. Smoke cleared, and the jungle was safe again. The trees swayed gently, thankful for their brave friends. That day, the animals learnt: when everyone helps, even small paws can save something big.

58. The Tickle Vine

Tommy the tiger was strolling through the jungle when he suddenly tripped over a twisty green vine. 'Oof!' he grunted, landing with a bump. But then—wiggle, wiggle! The vine moved! It slid up and tickled his tummy. Tommy let out a huge roar... of laughter! 'Hahahaha!' he giggled, rolling around in the grass. More vines joined in, gently tickling his paws and belly. Soon, tears of laughter rolled down his cheeks. Birds and monkeys peeked through the trees, curious about the noise. Seeing Tommy laugh so much, they all burst into giggles too. The jungle echoed with happy chuckles. That day, Tommy learnt that even a tumble can lead to tickly fun and a jungle full of joy.

59. Jungle Trickster Spirit

Milo the monkey was hungry for bananas. But when he reached his favourite banana tree—oh no! They were gone! 'Who took them?" he cried. Just then, a swirl of leaves danced past. A cheeky jungle spirit appeared, grinning behind a colourful mask. It held a banana, waved, and zipped away! Milo laughed and chased after him, swinging through trees and leaping over logs. The spirit giggled and tossed bananas like breadcrumbs through the jungle. Other animals joined the fun, slipping and sliding after the trail. At last, the spirit vanished in a puff of leaves. Bananas rained down. Milo shared them with everyone. That day, the jungle learnt that a little mischief can lead to lots of laughter.' into the following illustration: rustic gouache thick-paint-style illustration

60. The Brave Mouse

In the heart of the jungle, a tiny mouse named Momo lived quietly under a big leaf. One sunny day, a giant crocodile crept out of the river, snapping its jaws. All the animals ran, but Momo didn't move. Instead, he climbed onto a rock, puffed out his chest, and let out the loudest squeaky roar he could! 'SQUEEEEEAK!' The crocodile froze, blinked, and then jumped back into the river with a splash. The jungle went silent. Then—cheers and claps! The animals rushed out, lifting Momo high. 'You scared him away!' they cried. That day, the jungle learnt that even the smallest voice can be the bravest roar when spoken at the right moment.

In a quiet jungle corner, when stars blinked softly above, Nini the snake felt lonely. He wasn't scary—just shy. Animals often ran when he slithered past. One evening, while Nini curled under a bush, he heard a sniffle. Luna the rabbit was lost and scared. Nini gently whispered, 'It's alright, I'm here.' Luna blinked and smiled. 'You're warm,' she whispered. Without a second thought, Nini wrapped around her like a blanket. They sat under the glowing moon, hearts thumping softly together. From that night on, Nini wasn't just a snake—he was Luna's best friend. And every creature in the jungle learnt: sometimes, the warmest hugs come from the most unexpected hearts.

62. Sharing the Mangoes

The sun shone bright over the jungle, and the mangoes were finally ripe! Miko the monkey was the first to spot them. 'Mango day!' he cheered, swinging through the trees. Soon, he was joined by Tia, the tigress, and her curious cub. 'Can we try one?' the cub asked shyly. Miko smiled. Even Tutu the turtle joined. Mr Parrot, too, and laughter echoed through the leaves. Everyone shared, and no one was left out. That day, the jungle learnt: the sweetest fruit is the joy of sharing.

63. Helping a Bird

One sunny morning, Ninu the blue elephant was exploring the jungle when he heard a tiny 'cheep!' Near a patch of daisies, he spotted a yellow chick in a nest, all alone. 'Hello, little one! Where's your mummy?' Ninu asked gently. The chick chirped sadly. Just then, Meera the peacock rushed over. 'There you are!' she cried. 'We've been looking everywhere!' The chick flapped with joy. Ninu trumpeted happily and helped lift the chick back into its nest with his trunk. Flowers danced, butterflies twirled, and the sun smiled down. That day, Ninu learnt: even small kindnesses can make big hearts even bigger. And the jungle whispered, 'Thank you, Ninu,' in every flutter and breeze.

64. The Nest Builders

One sunny morning, Lily the rabbit, Toby the tree frog, and Rolo the lizard found a bundle of twigs beside the stream. 'A nest!' squeaked Rolo. 'Let's build it together!' smiled Lily. They gathered leaves, twigs, and soft feathers. Lily wove, Toby pressed, and Rolo tucked each piece with his tiny claws. The jungle birds watched curiously. 'Almost done!' cheered Toby, hopping excitedly. Finally, a perfect nest sat by the water, warm and cosy. A tired little bird fluttered down, chirped gratefully, and curled inside. Lily, Toby, and Rolo cheered loudly, clapping paws and sticky feet. That day, they learnt that the best homes aren't built alone—but with helping hands, careful claws, and cheerful teamwork.

65. Finding Mummy Lion

In a quiet corner of the jungle, a little lion cub sat alone beneath a tree, his ears drooping and his tail curled tight. Roarrr... he cried out, his tiny voice echoing through the trees. But no one answered. He sniffled and let out one more hopeful roar. Suddenly, from far away, a deep and loving roar rolled back through the forest — Mummy! the cub gasped. He leapt to his paws and dashed through the bushes, over logs, and past startled birds. There she was — Mummy Lion! With open paws and a warm smile. They hugged tight as the sun peeked through the trees. That day, the jungle felt whole again.

66. The Clean River

One morning, Bruno the bear looked sadly at the muddy river. 'It used to sparkle,' he sighed. Tara the panther dipped her paw and frowned. 'We should clean it!' 'Together!' grinned Felix the fox, grabbing a rake. With brooms, buckets, and giggles, they got to work. Bruno swept the banks, Tara scooped out soggy leaves, and Felix fished out twigs with his rake. Sunlight glimmered on the water as bubbles danced and splashed. Soon, the river was clear, cool, and full of sparkle again. 'Look!' cheered Bruno. 'The fish are back too!' That day, they learnt that even a big mess can be fixed—with teamwork, care, and a little bit of bubbly fun.

67. Painting a Chameleon

One morning, Chester the chameleon felt gloomy and grey. 'Where did your colours go?' gasped Max the monkey. 'I feel invisible,' Chester sighed. 'Not for long!' chirped Pippa the parrot, grabbing a paintbrush. Out came paint pots—yellow, red, blue, and green! Max dabbed spongey blobs, Pippa splashed spots, and Fergie the frog carefully patted patterns. Chester giggled as bright colours danced across his skin—zigzags, polka dots, even a flower on his tail! When they were done, Chester wasn't just colourful—he was spectacular. The jungle burst with claps and giggles. That day, Chester learnt that friends don't just see you—they help you shine. And sometimes, a little splash of paint brings back a whole rainbow of smiles.

68. The Chocolate Queen

Cici Crow lived in the tallest tree in the jungle. Her feathers were scruffy, her beak was crooked, and the other animals often whispered, 'Ugly crow!' behind her back. But Cici didn't cry. She baked. In her nest, she stirred cocoa beans, jungle berries, and sweet nectar into little chocolate delights. One sunny day, she quietly left a basket of chocolates near the riverbank. Elephant tasted one. 'Delicious!' he trumpeted. Soon, the whole jungle was nibbling and munching. 'Who made these?' asked Tiger. Cici stepped out shyly. Silence. Then Rabbit blushed. 'We were wrong,' she whispered. That evening, the animals built her a beautiful treehouse bakery. From then on, Cici was known as the Sweetheart of the Jungle.

69. Mind your Manners

Max the porcupine wasn't mean—just a little prickly and forgetful. One snowy morning, he barged past Bunny, snatched Mouse's snowball, and ignored Fox's cheerful 'hello'. 'Oops,' mumbled Max, seeing his friends frown. Bunny stepped forward kindly. 'Max, good friends share, listen, and say sorry too.' Max's cheeks blushed pink. He bowed low and softly said, 'I'm sorry.' Then he helped Mouse rebuild the snowball, shared berries from his bag, and even told a silly joke. Everyone burst into laughter. That day, Max learnt that manners weren't just rules—they were tiny acts of kindness that made everyone feel warm, even in the snow. And from that moment, Max didn't just look sharp—he acted sweet too.

43

70. Saving the Garden

One rainy morning, the jungle garden was in trouble. Puddles grew bigger, and the poor flowers were drowning! Water rushed through the flower beds, turning them into muddy puddles. 'We must help!' cried the little white rabbits. Grabbing their tiny spades, they began digging neat little drains. Bit by bit, the water trickled away through the channels they made. The sun peeked through the clouds, warming the earth. Slowly, the flowers lifted their heads — pink, yellow, and smiling once again. 'Thank you, bunnies!' giggled the blossoms. The garden sparkled, clean and happy. The rabbits flopped beside the flowers, tired but proud. That day, they learnt that a little teamwork could turn a flood into a blooming miracle.

71. The Ant Bridge

The rain had turned the jungle path into a muddy river. A tiny turtle stood at the edge, looking worried. He needed to get across, but the water was too fast for his little legs. Just then, a trail of ants marched up. 'We'll help!' they chirped. Working together, they carried a big green leaf and stretched it across the stream. Slowly and carefully, the turtle stepped onto the leaf. The ants held it steady from both sides, their tiny feet gripping the mud. With each step, the turtle smiled wider. At last, he reached the other side safe and dry. 'Thank you, friends!' he beamed. That day, the jungle learnt — even the smallest can build the biggest bridges.

72. Singing with the Parrots

Early one morning, Ruby the rabbit stood in the middle of the jungle and took a deep breath. Then she sang. Her big voice bounced through the trees like sunshine on leaves. One by one, colourful parrots poked out of the branches.

'Squawk!' 'Tweet!' 'La-la-la!' They joined Ruby's tune, filling the air with chirps and trills. The jungle woke up, delighted. Leaves rustled in rhythm, monkeys tapped on tree trunks, and butterflies danced mid-air. Even sleepy Sloth swayed gently. Ruby twirled, giggling, as parrots swooped around her in harmony. That day, music stitched them all together — feathers, fur, and fun. The jungle didn't just sing — it danced with joy.

Deep in the jungle, hidden behind tall vines, was a very special school — the Secret Survival School. It was run by Professor Owl, the wisest bird in the forest. Each day, baby parrots gathered on soft grass as Owl pointed to drawings on a jungle chalkboard. 'Today, we learn how to fly safely!' he hooted, adjusting his tiny glasses. The parrots listened carefully, eyes wide and feathers fluffed. They practiced flapping, gliding, and even crash-landing gently on leaves. Owl taught tree-climbing, storm-hiding, and how to spot tasty fruits. The little ones chirped with excitement. It wasn't just a school — it was their jungle family. And every lesson helped them soar a little braver, a little higher.

74. Weaving Vines

Ellie the elephant had a clever idea. She looked around the jungle and saw long vines hanging from the trees. 'Hmm,' she smiled, 'these would make perfect swings!' With her strong trunk, she carefully twisted and braided the vines into ropes. One by one, she tied them to sturdy branches and made cosy wooden seats. Her friends gathered around—bunny, duckling, squirrel, and bear—all giggling with excitement. Ellie gave a gentle push, and off they swung, higher and higher, squealing with joy! The jungle echoed with laughter and creaky vine swishes. That day, Ellie learnt that giving joy is just as fun as swinging—and her woven vines became the happiest playground in the forest.

75. The Jungle Paint Party

It was the silliest day the jungle had ever seen! Crows swooped in with pots of bright jungle paint, and before anyone could blink, SPLAT! A blue splash landed on a zebra's ear. SPLASH! Pink stripes danced across another's tail. Zebras laughed so hard they wobbled. The crows flapped joyfully, tossing colours into the sky like fireworks. The trees wore polka dots, the grass turned rainbow, and even the sun seemed to giggle behind a splash of orange. By the end, no one remembered who started it — only that laughter echoed through the leaves. That day, they learnt it's okay to be messy, as long as you're messy together.

76. Drumming in the Jungle

Ayesha couldn't believe her eyes when she saw the forest come alive. At first, she thought she was dreaming — but everything was real. Right in front of her, Tommy the turtle was drumming on big jungle leaves with his tiny feet. Tap! Tum! Tap! The sound echoed like magic. The ground thumped gently in time. A fox twirled, a lion cub jumped with glee, and even the shy koala clapped its paws to the beat. Ayesha sat in the middle, eyes wide, as the animals danced wildly around her. The jungle sparkled with colour and sound. That moment, she realised: this wasn't a dream. She had stepped into a magical forest — one where rhythm made the trees smile.

77. The Talking Wind

One quiet afternoon, a soft whoosh swept through the jungle. The little crocodile cub perked up his ears. The wind didn't just blow — it whispered. 'Adventure waits ahead...' it murmured as it danced through the trees. Leaves twirled, vines shivered, and colourful petals rode the air like tiny kites. The cub looked around — but no one else heard. The wind swirled again, tickling his snout. 'Come along!' it teased, tossing a trail of red and green leaves. His eyes sparkled. With a wide grin, he took a step forward, following the breeze. That day, he learnt that some adventures don't shout — they whisper gently through the wind, just loud enough for brave hearts to hear.

78. The Tree Climbers

Penny the parrot flapped joyfully onto the jungle swing. 'Watch this!' she chirped. Bluebird followed, and together they swung high and fast, their laughter fluttering through the trees. Just below, two kittens sat cuddled close beneath the rainbow-covered branches. They didn't swing or chirp — they just watched. But oh, how they giggled! Every flap, every silly spin, every leaf that flew made their eyes sparkle brighter. The parrots' joy danced like sunlight, and soon the kittens' purrs matched the rhythm. That day, they learnt something beautiful — you don't have to be in the air to feel lifted. When laughter is shared, happiness spreads. It's quiet, it's gentle... and it's gloriously contagious.

79. The Crocodile Who Scored

Crispin the crocodile loved video games. He played all day—zoom, zap, pow! But homework? Never! His dad roared, 'Enough! You're turning your brain to jelly!' Crispin rolled his eyes, but one day, a surprise test popped up in class. He hadn't even opened his book! That night, something strange happened—he studied! Just a little... then a little more. The next week, the teacher announced, 'Top marks... Crispin!' The class gasped. His cheeks went pink. He even got a shiny award sticker. Back home, his dad blinked and said, 'Well done, son.' Crispin smiled, tucked his game away, and whispered, 'Learning feels kinda cool.' From that day on, he balanced games with books—and life got way more epic.

80. Climbing High Trees

In the middle of the jungle, a little lizard spotted the tallest tree he had ever seen. 'I wonder what's up there,' he whispered. With a brave heart and sticky toes, he began to climb — higher than the bushes, past birds' nests, above fluttering butterflies. The air got cooler, the wind whispered louder, but the lizard didn't stop. At last, he reached the top branch. Wow! From up there, the whole jungle stretched below like a leafy sea. But best of all — across the sky arched a giant, glowing rainbow! Colours danced in the clouds. The little lizard grinned. That day, he learnt: when you dare to climb higher, the world rewards you with wonder.

81. The Dancing friends

In a quiet part of the jungle, where the trees whispered softly and roses bloomed beautifully, Finny Fox and Dinah Deer shared a special moment. They laughed — not loud, but the kind of laugh that tickled the heart. A breeze rustled the petals around them, and suddenly, Finny twirled! Dinah followed with a leap. Together, they danced between the roses, paws and hooves stirring fallen petals into the air. Their joy filled the glade with warmth. The jungle paused to watch — not with noise, but in still, smiling silence. That day, the roses didn't just bloom, they danced too. Because when friends move with laughter, even the flowers remember the rhythm.

82. Kora loves dancing

Kora the kitten loved to dance — twirling, tapping, leaping with joy! Her paws moved like sunshine, and her whiskers wiggled to the beat. One day, as she spun beneath a leafy tree, a curious rabbit stopped to watch... and bounced along. Then a fox joined, wagging his tail in rhythm. A tiger tapped his big paws, and even a shy donkey gave a joyful wiggle. Soon, laughter echoed through the jungle — the trees swayed, the vines shimmied, and animals danced everywhere! "Let's have a Jungle Flash Dance!" Kora meowed. And they did! Now, the jungle is buzzing with music and excitement. Everyone's practising for the Jungle Dance International Show — all inspired by one little kitten who danced with her heart.

83. The Cheeky Parrot

In the golden morning light, Polly the parrot perched on a rock beside the mighty lion. With a twinkle in her eye, she puffed out her feathers and squawked, 'ROAR!' The sound echoed across the savannah. The lion's eyes went wide. 'Did you just roar like me?' he gasped. Polly nodded proudly. The lion blinked... then burst into the loudest, jolliest laugh the jungle had heard! He laughed so hard he rolled onto the ground. Polly joined in, flapping and giggling. Soon, other animals peeked out, chuckling too. That day, they all learned: it's okay to joke, even with the king — especially if it ends in shared laughter and a new friendship.

84. The Happy Cat

In the heart of the jungle, where butterflies danced and flowers bloomed in every colour, lived a little white cat named Miu. She was just three years old and wore a yellow dress covered in white polka dots. With wide eyes and open arms, she stood in a field full of blossoms, smiling so big that even the sun seemed to shine brighter. Birds chirped above her, bees hummed nearby, and the grass tickled her toes. 'I'm happy,' she whispered, spinning with joy. 'Truly, happily jungle-happy!' Miu didn't need toys or treats — her friends, the flowers, and the breeze were enough. That day, the jungle echoed her laughter, as if it, too, smiled back at her.

85. The Jungle Friendship

Deep in the jungle, a big green monster peeked out from behind a bush. He looked shy but hopeful. Nearby, a cheerful parrot was singing on a branch. 'Hello,' the monster said softly. The parrot fluttered down and smiled. 'Wanna be friends?' From that moment, everything changed. They laughed, played, and shared juicy jungle fruits. To celebrate their new friendship, they exchanged gifts. The monster gave the parrot a beautiful flower scarf, soft and colourful. The parrot gifted the monster a leafy hat that fit just right. They looked at each other and cheered, 'Fabulous!' That day, the jungle buzzed with happiness — proof that friendship blooms when hearts are open and gifts come wrapped in love.

86. The Moving River

One morning, the jungle animals woke up to find the river had taken a new path! It twisted and turned through the meadows, bubbling with excitement. The old crossing was gone! 'Oh no!' cried Rabbit. 'How will we visit our friends now?' Fox grinned. 'Let's build a bridge!' Together, they gathered planks, vines, and stones. Squirrel tied ropes, Otter dragged logs, and even the birds helped drop twigs into place. The water splashed and sparkled as laughter filled the air. Soon, bridges crossed the new river bend — some wobbly, some fancy, all full of fun. That day, they didn't just build crossings — they built giggles, teamwork, and a brand-new path to play.

54

87. The Jungle Hide-and-Seek

The jungle was full of giggles that morning. 'Ready or not, here I come!' shouted Monkey, eyes squeezed shut behind his paws. Tiger tiptoed away and slipped behind a curtain of thick, leafy vines. He tried to hold his breath, but a giggle bubbled up. Heehee! Monkey's ears twitched. He peeked through one vine... then another... and there — two orange paws, a twitchy tail, and a very wiggly giggle! 'Found you!' Monkey cheered. Tiger burst out laughing, tumbling into the sunlight. The vines swayed as the game began again. That day, the jungle learnt: the best hiding places come with laughter, and every giggle is a clue waiting to be discovered.

88. The Christmas Crocodile

In a bend of the jungle river lived Crispo the crocodile—old, rich, and always grumpy. But this year, as cold winds blew, Crispo noticed shivering animals with no coats, empty bellies, and sad faces. 'This won't do,' he muttered. He paddled off to the market and returned with carts full of warm scarves, rice sacks, honey jars, and even toys! On Christmas Eve, Crispo invited everyone to his riverside—monkeys, moles, even a shy snake. 'From now on,' he smiled, 'you'll have food, clothes—and jobs! Let's celebrate together!' They danced, sang, and feasted under twinkling fireflies. That night, the jungle wasn't just warm—it sparkled with joy. And Crispo? He wasn't grumpy anymore—he was jolly.

89. Emu Smoothie Stand

Under the warm jungle sun, Era the emu opened her colourful smoothie stand. She wore a bright smile and fluffed her feathers as she blended bananas, berries, and jungle mangoes with a whirr! Bear arrived first, slurping a minty green mix with a happy sigh. Penguin waddled up next, sipping a tangy orange delight with a grin. A cheerful toucan tapped his beak on the counter, waiting for his fruity treat. The stand buzzed with giggles and straw slurps as friends from all over the jungle lined up for Era's famous drinks. That day, no one argued, no one hurried — they simply sipped, smiled, and enjoyed the sweet joy of sharing smoothies under the sunshine.

90. Animals Try Human Jobs

In the middle of the jungle, something strange was happening. Parrot wore a little postman hat and delivered letters, squawking, 'Mail for Monkey!' Tiger put on glasses, picked up a chalk, and taught young cubs the alphabet. Bear opened a bakery, proudly icing cakes with his big furry paws. Giraffe became a window cleaner for the tallest trees! Every animal had a job, and they took it very seriously — even if they looked quite silly. The jungle roared with laughter and applause. 'Who needs humans when we've got talent right here?' giggled Monkey, filming everything on his coconut camera. That day, the animals learnt it's fun to try something new — even if your paws aren't made for post!

91. The Baby Gorilla and Kitten

In the heart of a quiet jungle clearing, a baby gorilla heard a soft meow. Curious, he followed the sound and found a shivering kitten with a blue ribbon around her neck. She looked up with wide eyes, and the gorilla's heart melted. He scooped her up gently with his big, furry arms. The kitten purred, nuzzling into his warm chest. The gorilla giggled, his smile stretching wide as banana leaves. Birds watched from branches, chirping happily at the odd but adorable friendship. From that day on, the two were inseparable — swinging together, sharing fruits, and curling up for naps. Everyone agreed: nothing is stronger than a gentle heart, especially one wrapped in fur and friendship.

92. Camping Under Stars

One calm night, the animals of the forest decided to camp. Raccoon pitched a tiny tent beside a pine tree, while Hedgehog rolled out a striped blanket. Owl flapped down to light the campfire with fireflies dancing in golden swirls. Rabbit roasted carrots on sticks, and Squirrel played soft lullabies on his leaf-flute. As the fire crackled and flickered, the sky turned velvet dark, scattered with twinkling stars. Each animal climbed into their tent, whispering goodnight. Even the crickets sang softly. When the moon rose high, the whole forest glowed gently — a magical, peaceful dreamland. That night, they learnt: the best stories are whispered under starry skies, with fireflies for lanterns and friendship for warmth.

93. The Friendship Bridge

One sunny morning, Lion sat happily at the centre of a little wooden bridge. Along came two giggly bunnies, hopping side by side. 'Hello!' said Lion with a big roar-grin. The bunnies froze—then burst into laughter! 'That roar sounded like a sneeze!' giggled one. Lion blinked, then chuckled too. He tried again: 'ROA—CHOO!' This time, even louder giggles filled the forest. Soon, all three were rolling with laughter, dangling their feet over the bridge. And even the river below seemed to giggle along with gentle splashes. That day, they discovered that a shared laugh on a little bridge can build the biggest friendship of all.

94. Singing Competition

In the heart of the jungle, a stage was built from logs and leaves. 'Tonight's the big singing contest!' hooted Owl, holding a microphone. Parrot strutted up first, feathers gleaming, and belted out a high-pitched song. 'Squaaawk!' The crowd cheered. Then Frog hopped on stage, cleared his throat, and sang a silly, wobbly tune. 'Ribbit-ribbit-reeeee!' Animals burst into giggles. Suddenly, fireflies floated up, blinking like shining musical notes, dancing in the air as applause. Parrot bowed with flair. Frog also joined in. Owl declared, 'Everyone wins when we sing from the heart!' That night, the jungle echoed with laughter, tunes, and friendship — proof that joy doesn't need perfect pitch, just a brave voice.

95. The Jungle Library

As the jungle fell quiet and the fireflies began to twinkle, a soft glow lit up beneath the big banyan tree. Three bright leaf-lamps hung from a branch, casting golden light onto a cosy clearing. Elephant gently opened a green book. Monkey, Squirrel, and Rabbit each had one too. 'Once upon a jungle...' the pages whispered. The animals sat in a circle, their eyes wide with wonder. Every night, they met in this secret nook to read together — stories of stars, rainbows, and brave little bugs. Even the trees leaned in to listen. That night, they learnt that the jungle's greatest treasure wasn't gold or bananas — it was the magic of stories, shared with friends.

96. The Rainbow After Rain

The rain had stopped at last. Drops still clung to the leaves, glittering like tiny diamonds. The jungle looked freshly washed, colours brighter, branches shinier. A hush filled the air — and then, a gasp! A glowing rainbow stretched across the sky, its colours dripping softly into each other like wet paint. 'Wow!' whispered Monkey. Parrot fluttered up for a closer look. Even sleepy Bear blinked in wonder. The trees seemed to lean into the colours, as if being hugged. Flowers opened wider. Puddles sparkled with rainbows of their own. The animals danced beneath the gentle arch. It felt like a promise — that after every storm, something magical would always follow. A jungle smile made of colour.

97. Planting a Friendship Tree

One sunny afternoon, the jungle animals gathered around a bare patch of soil. 'Let's grow something beautiful — together!' said Bunny, holding a shiny seed. Elephant dug a gentle hole with his trunk. Piggy and Hedgehog joined in, their paws and noses soon covered in warm, squishy mud. Everyone giggled. They placed the seed in the ground and gave it a soft pat. 'Grow big and strong,' whispered Piggy. Days passed, and one morning, a green sprout peeked out. Soon, colourful blossoms bloomed all around. Their tiny seed had become a huge, leafy Friendship Tree! It stood tall, full of love, laughter, and muddy pawprints — proof that when friends plant joy together, it grows forever.

98. Dream Sharing Spot

Beneath a wise old banyan tree, animals gathered every night. Its roots curled like a giant nest, and its branches stretched up to kiss the sky. As moonlight danced on the leaves, each friend took turns whispering their dreams. Hedgehog wished to fly. Mouse dreamed of a cheese castle. Rabbit wanted to visit his grandparents. Fox longed to write a book. Their voices were soft, full of wonder. Above them, the stars blinked gently, as if nodding in approval. The night sky listened closely, painted in deep indigo and stardust. No dream was too silly, no whisper too small. In that quiet spot, under the tree's embrace, every hope found a home in the stars.

99. The Brave Little Rabbit

Deep in the jungle, a loud rumble shook the ground. A log had fallen across the river, trapping the animals on one side. Everyone panicked. Tiger growled, Bear cried, Monkey fretted, and even Elephant looked worried. Then came a tiny squeak. Rabbit stepped forward. 'I'll help!' he said, eyes shining with courage. He scurried through the narrowest gaps, tugged at vines, and chewed through just the right spot. Crack! The log shifted, and water flowed again. The animals gasped, then roared with joy. Rabbit climbed onto a stone, puffing with pride. The jungle echoed with cheers. That night, they all learned that bravery isn't about size. It's about the heart.

100. The Jungle Guardian

Once, a young child wandered into the jungle — not to take, but to help. He bandaged bird wings, planted baby trees, and even pulled a thorn from Lion's paw. Word spread quickly. 'He's one of us!' chirped Parrot. One glowing morning, the animals gathered beneath the ancient tree. Monkey giggled with excitement, Bunny hummed a tune, and Lion stepped forward with a golden crown made from jungle vines. Gently, he placed it on the child's head. 'From today, you are the Jungle Guardian,' he roared. The jungle burst into cheers! Fireflies lit up like stars, and the vines shimmered in gold. And from that moment on, the child sat proudly — a friend, a helper, and a true guardian forever.

101. Panda Hug

Deep in the quiet bamboo forest, a baby panda clambered through the ferns with giggly paws and curious eyes. 'Mama!' he squeaked, tumbling forward. His mother turned with a warm smile, arms open wide. With a soft plop, the baby landed in her lap, and the biggest panda hug wrapped them both in safety and love. All around, tall trees watched gently, and the breeze tiptoed softly between the trunks. They didn't speak much — they didn't need to. Their eyes sparkled, cheeks nuzzled close. That hug said everything. Because sometimes, the happiest place in the whole jungle... is someone's arms.